Why do we need Art?

What do we gain by being creative? And other Big Questions

Michael Rosen & Annemarie Young

WAYLAND
www.waylandbooks.co.uk

For everyone in the NHS, and all workers who have kept us going during these difficult times.
For Emma, Elsie and Emile (M.R.)
For Anthony and Ben (A.Y.)

First published in Great Britain in 2020 by Wayland
Michael Rosen and Annemarie Young have asserted their rights to be identified as the Authors of the Work.
Text copyright © Michael Rosen and Annemarie Young, 2020
Contributor text Copyright: pp 14-15 Andria Zafirakou's text © Andria Zafirakou, 2020; pp20-21 Lemn Sissay's text © Lemn Sissay, 2020; pp26-27 Preti Taneja's text © Preti Taneja, 2020; pp30-31 Peter Beard's text © Peter Beard, 2020; pp36-37 Mathilda Crompton's text © Mathilda Crompton, 2020; page 33 Meri Wells' text © Meri Wells, 2020; pp42-43 Kate Clanchy's text © Kate Clanchy, 2020

Editor: Nicola Edwards
Design: Rocket Design (East Anglia) Ltd
Cover artwork by Oli Frape
Lion artwork on page 20 by Giles Aston

ISBN 978 1 5263 1258 7 (hb) 978 1 5263 1259 4 (pb)

Wayland, an imprint of
Hachette Children's Group
Part of Hodder and Stoughton
Carmelite House
50 Victoria Embankment
London EC4Y 0DZ

An Hachette UK Company
www.hachette.co.uk
www.hachettechildrens.co.uk

Printed and bound in Dubai

We would like to thank:

Andria Zafirakou, Lemn Sissay, Preti Taneja, Peter Beard, Mathilda Crompton, Meri Wells and Kate Clanchy for their contributions.

Thanks to the following for sharing their experiences with us in different ways, and to all who have contributed to the book in some way: Akram Khan, Ai Weiwei's Studio, Steve McQueen, Sally Peters, Sonia Boyce, Olafur Eliasson, Rufus Hound, Shazia Mirza, Will Todd and George the Poet.

Anthony Robinson, for his perceptive and helpful comments throughout the project.

And a big thank you to our excellent editor, Nicola Edwards, for her invaluable input, as always.

Picture acknowledgements:
Alamy: Alpha Historica 5l; don john red 12; Science History Images 25b. Hamish Brown 20. Paul Cochrane 45l. Julia Forster 36. Getty Images: Timothy A Clary 23; Martha Holmes/The LIFE Picture Collection 16b; Ipsumpix 29; Mike Marsland/Wire Image 18; Gjon Mili 9c. Ben Gold 26. Courtesy of Goldsmiths, University of London back cover l, 10. Beth Halliday 40. Benji Johnson 41. Kunsthorisches Museum/Google Cultural Institute. PD/Wikimedia Commons 13t. Graham CopeKoga 30; John Millar 31; Rory Mulvey 34. Andre Natta/Wikimedia Commons CCA 2 9t. Markus Ortner/Wikimedia Commons CCSA 2.5 19. Reuters 7. Anthony Robinson back cover r, 11, 37b. Shutterstock: Amani A 28; Esther Barry 35; Elnutr 13b; Featureflash Photo Agency 22, 24, 38; Sheila Fitzgerald 32; Marcus Gebauer 6b; Chris Halberg 45r; Charles Martin Hatch 4; Kim Jihyun 25c; Mike O 21; Milan M 5r; Giannis Papanikos 33; Andrey Popov 16t; Prisma mountainpix 6t; Lev Radin 9b; Arporn Seemaroj palette motif throughout. Idil Sukan 39. Pete Telfer 37t. George Torode 42. Varkey Foundation 14.

Text acknowledgements:
p8 Sally Peters, Speak Art Loud, (https://speakartloud.wordpress.com)
p43 Mohamed Assaf's poem published in England, Poems from a School, (Picador)

Andria Zafirakou and Artists in Residence (https://www.artistsinresidence.org.uk)
Lemn Sissay (https://www.lemnsissay.com)
Preti Taneja (http://www.preti-taneja.co.uk)
Peter Beard (http://www.peterbeard.co.uk)
Ai Weiwei (https://www.aiweiwei.com)
Akram Khan (https://www.akramkhancompany.net)
Olafur Eliasson (https://www.olafureliasson.net) Also https://www.netflix.com/gb/title/80057883
Meri Wells (http://meriwells.co.uk)
Shazia Mirza (https://www.shazia-mirza.com)
Will Todd (https://willtodd.co.uk)
George the Poet (https://www.georgethepoet.com).
Kate Clanchy on Twitter (https://bit.ly/3fmXGi9)
Sonia Boyce (https://bit.ly/2OJPDQz)

Contents

What is this book about? _____ 4

What is art for? _____ 6

Why do we need art? _____ 8

My experience: Michael Rosen _____ 10

My experience: Annemarie Young _____ 11

Where do artists come from? _____ 12

My experience: Andria Zafirakou _____ 14

How is art transformative? _____ 16

Where do we find art? _____ 18

My experience: Lemn Sissay _____ 20

Do you need training to become an artist? _____ 22

What use is the imagination? _____ 24

My experience: Preti Taneja _____ 26

What do we gain by being creative? _____ 28

My experience: Peter Beard _____ 30

Can art speak truth to power? _____ 32

Can art change anything? _____ 34

My experience: Mathilda Crompton and Meri Wells _____ 36

Is comedy art? _____ 38

Why do we create music? _____ 40

My experience: Kate Clanchy _____ 42

What do you think? _____ 44

Over to you! _____ 46

Glossary and further information _____ 47

Index _____ 48

What is this book about?

What comes to mind when you see the word 'art'? This interesting question is especially relevant for this book. Perhaps you think that art is only found in art galleries, and that's not for you. But art, and other products of the imagination, are all around us – look at the web pages you visit, the covers of the books you read, the images on the music you download, cartoons, graphic novels, your last birthday card, cereal packets, your bed covers, the posters on your wall. All that is art, and we're going to have a look at what it means to us.

What do we mean by art?

Art takes many forms and, as you'll see, what we mean by art is not just the kind you find in museums and galleries, or what you might think of as literature. We use the term in its widest sense, and you'll see that art and creativity encompass many different forms and ideas: music, film, dance, theatre, pottery, poetry, fiction, architecture,

design, crafts, even gardening and cooking – anything, in fact, where human beings use their imagination to create things, to transform material or ideas, from one thing into another. We'll talk about science, too, and get you to think about how much creativity matters in science. Without creativity there would be no internet or phones, no music or television; none of the things we take for granted.

This sculpture, by Maggi Hambling, is called 'The Scallop'. You can enjoy exploring its surfaces, and if you want to think about it, you could think of shellfish, the tide, or the sun as it shines on the silvery surface, or you can think of whatever you want.

How does the book work?

Our aim in this book is to get you to think for yourselves, and to express yourselves too. We'll raise lots of questions, such as: Who are artists? Do you need training to become an artist? Why do we need art? What use is the imagination? Can art change anything?

Of course, we couldn't possibly fit into this one book all the information you need in order to answer all the questions, so we'll provide you with some information and tell you what other people, working in a range of art forms, have thought and written about these and many other, related questions.

We'll also ask you to find out more about some of the issues raised by the questions, and how they relate to you, and we'll suggest things you might want to do to explore your own creativity.

The people in the book

We'll tell you about ourselves, and what art means to us. You will also hear from seven people — award-winning art teacher Andria Zafirakou, poet and writer Lemn Sissay, the poet, writer and teacher Kate Clanchy, writer, film-maker and teacher Preti Taneja, ceramicists and sculptors Peter Beard and Meri Wells, and young artist Mathilda Crompton — who will discuss their own experiences and thoughts about art. In addition, there are quotes from a wide variety of artists spread throughout the book.

The scientist Albert Einstein talked a lot about creativity and the links between imaginative inquiry and scientific discovery. It was his birthday when this photo was taken and he was in a playful mood!

> "Creativity is contagious.
> Pass it on."
>
> *Albert Einstein*

What is art for?

You might think this is a strange question to ask because we are so used to art as a fundamental part of all cultures and societies. Art has been found that dates back many thousands of years. For example, archaeologists found this flute in a cave in Germany. It is made from the bone taken from a vulture's wing – so the people who made it must have made music, as well as making what might have been a decorative object.

The flute was made during the Ice Age, 35,000 years ago.

Art around the world

Art has different meanings in different cultures. For example, for the indigenous people of Australia, art plays a very important role, and is a manifestation of their beliefs and culture.

Two other cultures where art plays a key part are Bhutan and the Ainu people of northern Japan.

Bhutan is a small kingdom in the Eastern Himalayas, where Buddhism is the main religion. The Buddhist tradition here means that art is an essential part of daily life. Objects for everyday use are still made as they were centuries ago, with traditional craft skills handed down through the generations. These include working in metal, wood, clay and bamboo.

The Aboriginal people used storytelling to convey their knowledge of the land, to talk about events and beliefs, and so preserve their culture through the generations. With no written language, they used symbols and images like these, drawn on rock walls.

For the Ainu, the indigenous people of Hokkaido in northern Japan, oral storytelling is used to pass on history, legends and their way of life. The stories are enhanced by music, songs and dance.

Why is creativity so important in times of crisis?

As we've been writing this book, the coronavirus pandemic has been sweeping across the world. While people have been confined to their homes, whether that's a room, a house or a flat, they have used art and creativity in all sorts of ways: to create stories, drawings, videos, internet group activities – to overcome isolation, show empathy and connect with families, friends and strangers.

Once we're over the worst of the pandemic, thinking creatively in all aspects of life –

personal relationships, society, government, the economy – is going to be crucial, as returning to exactly how things were before will be out of the question. People have already demonstrated how important creativity is, by finding new ways to access the things they need, setting up support groups and so on.

Creative thinking is going to be needed in relation to global issues too, especially as the climate crisis becomes more acute. The lockdowns all over the world have shown us what it's like when there are many fewer cars on the road and planes in the sky to pollute the air. What can be done to make this reduction in air pollution and gas emissions more permanent? It's going to take a great deal of creative thinking to come up with solutions.

Photography is an art form that can make us think. The dramatic improvement in air quality can be seen in these photos taken before and during the lockdown in 2020 in Delhi, India.

Why do we need art?

Sally Peters, founder of SpeakArtLoud, has had a long career in public service and higher education. She's particularly interested in the relationship between art and community development and has given a lot of thought to why we need art. Here are her five reasons:

1 Art is a natural human behaviour

Children the world over instinctively make things. Every culture has art, just as they have language and laughter. We need art because it makes us complete human beings.

2 Art is communication

Art, like language, is a medium to express ideas and to share information. Art offers us a method to communicate what we may not necessarily fully understand or know how to express. We need art in order to have a full range of expression.

3 Art is healing

Creating or experiencing art can relax and sooth us, or it may enliven and stimulate us. The process of creating art engages both the body and the mind and provides us with time to look inward and reflect. We need art to keep healthy.

4 Art tells our story

Art documents events and experiences and allows us a richer understanding of history. Art reflects cultural values, beliefs and identity and helps to preserve the many different communities that make up our world. Art chronicles our own lives and experiences over time. We need art to understand and to share our individual and shared history.

5 Art is a shared experience

The creation of art is a collective activity. Art forms such as dance, theatre and choir all require a group of artists and an audience. Even the solitary painter or poet relies upon the craft of the paint-maker or bookbinder to help create art, and an audience to experience it. We need art to keep us connected.

Art as a collaborative activity

We tend to think of artists working on their own, but art can be made by groups of people working together, as well as by individuals.

There are examples of people collaborating to make different forms of art, in many cultures and places. Here are three.

The Master Quilters of Gee's Bend, Alabama

Gee's Bend is a rural community, originally settled by freed slaves in Alabama in the United States, recognised for its remarkable quilts. The tradition of quilting is passed from mother to daughter. The quilts tell the stories of the community, and also express the individuality of the makers (right).

Pablo Picasso and Gjon Mili: Drawing with Pure Light

In 1949, *Life* magazine photographer Gjon Mili visited Pablo Picasso to take some pictures of the artist's creative process. The two decided to collaborate on exploring the possibilities of painting with light. Picasso used the flash of a light as though it were paint, with the air as the canvas, and Mili photographed the results, producing thirty images, including Picasso's signature and a bull-shaped light trail (see right) that remained invisible until the photographs were developed.

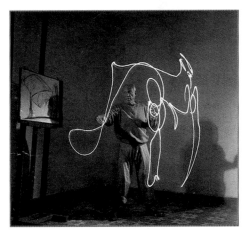

Making music

Many musicians work collaboratively to make their music. Bands often work together from the early stages of an album, playing around with ideas for lyrics or tunes and creating the whole. The Beatles worked this way in the sixties, and the American group Haim work like that today. The singer Rihanna (right) often collaborates with other singers, as she did with Pharrell Williams on the single *Lemon*.

My experience

Michael Rosen

I write poems and stories. I often perform these in schools and at festivals. My son Joe films me performing my poems and stories to create a YouTube Channel. I love doing all this. It makes me happy and I can see that many people seem to enjoy reading what I write or seeing me do my shows. I believe that as I write I learn things about myself, the people around me and the world we live in. That's because I think writing is like exploring: peering into my own mind and looking closely at what I can see and hear in order to find out how all this works.

From imitation to invention

I started doing some of this when I was about 12. I wrote poems and stories as part of school work, but I also joined an acting club where we could practise performing in different ways. Around the age of 15 or 16 I got the 'bug': I had read some poems and stories and simply said to myself, 'I would like to write like that'. And I did! It was partly imitation, partly invention. What I wrote was similar but not the same.

Later, I went to university and spent a lot of my time reading, writing, acting and directing shows. I think that this time gave me a springboard for me to feel confident about writing and performing.

What I write about

I often write about my family and I like creating scenes which are exaggerated, as with my 'No breathing' piece about a teacher who – supposedly – didn't let us breathe in class! I enjoy experimenting with styles of writing, sometimes rhyming, sometimes using repetition that an audience can join in with. I like variation of mood: crazy, sad, exaggerated, odd and so on.

I believe that performance is important because it re-connects words with our bodies, just as it was for ancient storytellers, or as it is for children before they learn to read. I work very hard on finding new ways to help audiences feel what I'm saying through what I do with my voice, face and movements.

"... writing is like exploring ..."

My experience

Annemarie Young

I hated art lessons in primary school because I just didn't think I could do it. I put too much effort into getting things 'right'. The only lessons I did enjoy were the ones where we played with paint.

Stories

I've always loved books and stories. My mother used to tell me traditional stories in French, and she bought me books to read. I still have my first copy of *Tom's Midnight Garden* by Philippa Pearce, the early books of Alan Garner and a host of other historical and fantasy novels, all of which I devoured. From reading these stories, and all those I read later, I decided that I wanted to write stories too.

I thought I wasn't creative enough

When I was young, I wanted to write the sorts of stories that I liked to read, but what I wrote was dry and boring, and not at all like the books I loved. I never seemed able to let my imagination explore the possibilities. So I gave up on the idea for a very long time. Then as part of my job, I was asked to try writing different kinds of stories – short, amusing books for children learning to read. And I found that I was good at those. I discovered that having constraints – like being given particular words or sounds to use in a story, or the form of a poem, as with haiku – can actually free up the imagination. I really enjoyed the challenge, especially having to think of stories with a funny ending. After the first one worked, I gained the confidence to keep going.

Now I write books like this one, as well as stories for young children and books that tell the true stories of refugee children, and of what it's like for Palestinian young people to live under occupation. I now know that I too can be creative.

I'd thought that I could only be a viewer, reader, listener, not a creator. But now I see that anyone can find their own way of creating something worthwhile, whatever field of art you're interested in.

> "... anyone can find their own way of creating something worthwhile ..."

Where do artists come from?

Artists are all around us. They are the people who write the music you like, make the films you see, write and illustrate the books you read. They are the designers of everything you use, the buildings you live in, the cars, buses, trains and planes you ride in.

You are an artist too: every time you doodle on a page, every time you tell a joke, you create something and use your mind and body to make a new or different thing, or way of communicating.

Of course, there are famous artists and we like to put their work on show in theatres, galleries, museums and libraries, and we study them in schools. This sometimes leads people into thinking that making art is 'posh' or that you have to have come from a posh background to do artistic things.

This is not true.

Many famous artists were ordinary people

First, we should remember that the big, grand places where art is put on show are often paid for by everyone out of our taxes: they belong to all of us, we can all go and visit, see the plays and listen to the music.

We should remember that some of the most famous artists of all time started out life as very ordinary people. William Shakespeare's father was a glove-maker living in a small market-town. Hans Christian Andersen was mostly brought up by his mother who was a washerwoman, living in a very small home in a country town. The parents of one of the greatest dancers and choreographers, Pina Bausch, ran a restaurant. Beyoncé's mother was a hairdresser and her father sold photocopiers. The father of one of the world's most famous fashion designers, Alexander McQueen (below), was a taxi driver and his mother was a teacher.

Let's look at what artists make their art from, and at what inspires them.

CHILDREN'S GAMES BY PIETER BREUGHEL THE ELDER

One of the best-known painters whose works are found in museums, is Pieter Breughel the Elder. He came from what we now call Holland. He painted the men, women and children he saw around him in the villages and towns, showing them working, playing, dancing, getting married. Sometimes he showed scenes of war, sometimes he put the people he knew into scenes from the Bible and famous myths. When you look at his pictures you see the lives, the dramas, the fun, the tragedies of everyday life.

Everyday things

Even the great buildings around us might be inspired by everyday things. The architect Zaha Hadid created buildings all over the world that look as if they have frozen something flowing, as if someone had poured them out of a jug and made them solid.

The South African architects Sumayya Vally, Sarah de Villiers and Amina Kaskar work with communities to create the kinds of buildings and spaces that people want – an architecture rooted in the lives of ordinary people.

Zaha Hadid was inspired by the shapes made when things in nature are half-way between solid and liquid. And she imitated them to make designs for her buildings all over the world, like this one in Baku, Azerbaijan.

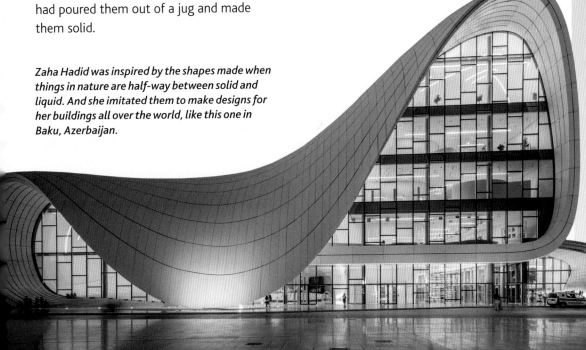

My experience

Andria Zafirakou

Andria Zafirakou, MBE, is an art and textiles teacher at Alperton Community School in Brent, London. She won the 2018 Global Teacher Prize, an award presented to an exceptional teacher who has made an outstanding contribution to their profession. Andria is passionate about changing lives through creativity. Using the US$1,000,000 prize money, she founded a charity called Artists in Residence (AiR) with the aim to improve arts education in schools.

Art: my great love and inspiration

Art always inspired me. In Year 1, I created a picture of my dad, and later my science teacher inspired me by buying my GCSE exam piece – that gave me such value and self-confidence. So now I buy pieces that I love from my students.

What do I want my students to gain from studying the arts?

I want them to create something which is truly theirs. I want them to experience having to make decisions. I want them to be curious, experimental, brave, but also to be social, communicative and collaborative. This is what I believe the arts can bring.

Why do we need art in schools?

Without it, students will never know who they are, or appreciate others. How does art do that? It starts like this: a child has a blank piece of paper in front of them, and they need to develop the skills and processes to create a piece. They have to make decisions, raise questions and deliberate. They'll make a mistake and decide not to rub it out but to keep it and develop it as part of the piece. All of that is a journey of discovering themselves. It's challenging – and there's no right or wrong.

It's being bold enough to make the first mark, whichever art form. When you see a young person perform in a production with others, you see them going through rehearsals with their peers – the discipline, timing, teamwork. The skills you develop during this process you never forget, always value and reflect on.

What do children lose if there is no art?

Joy, freedom, social skills, personal achievement. Some might say that achievement comes from doing something analytical, like science or maths, or interpreting history. But I'm talking about personal achievement. Even, for example, making a cake. That gives them pride and confidence – two of the most important things that can help children to thrive.

And something else: in the art room you can't see the disabilities of children who have special educational needs, or social or emotional problems. They can be as good as anyone else. And that's the power of the arts. These are the children who need it most. If they grow up with the skills art can give them, they will be made resilient, and they can integrate successfully.

Discipline and rigour

I have high expectations of my students, and the quality I get from them is high. There's structure, expectation, demand. There are two sides: academic and making. There's extraordinary discipline in mastering a technique, and academic rigour in finding out about artists and art movements, cultural influences and historical context, and in being critical. To master painting, one of the things you have to learn is to mix paints. The practical skills take years of practice.

We use art to unlock the students' creativity and confidence. Teenagers these days have a fear of being wrong in front of their peers, they think they always have to be right. We help them to accept, then improve and build on their mistakes. To learn from, rather than being afraid of, their mistakes. And to recognise that there's more than one solution to any problem.

My message to those in charge of education

Be brave and acknowledge that not everything that can be measured is important. And that things like inspiration, joy, fun, self-awareness, self-development *are* important, and not measurable in exams!

Artists in Residence is a charity founded to support schools and communities, where the arts aren't necessarily thriving, but are needed. Andria told us: "I've seen the power of connecting and the really transformational effect of a young person speaking to an artist or a designer. That collaboration, that communication, that's now their role model. And young people need good role models. They need that inspiration: 'I want to be like her, like him'. That's what Artists in Residence does."

" ... pride and confidence – two of the most important things that can help children to thrive."

How is art transformative?

There are two 'ends' to art. One end is the making, the other end is the receiving. On the making end, we have, for example, dancing, singing, painting, writing, acting. On the receiving end we have, for example, reading what's written, seeing what's been painted, watching what's being danced, hearing what's being sung, and so on.

At both ends, something gets transformed, meaning that there is change. The artist transforms something to make the art. The person (or people) on the receiving end are transformed by what they see, hear or read. A connection is made. Both ends need each other for this transformation to be complete.

Video gaming creates a connection between the players and the artists who designed the game.

Physical transformation

For a start, a lot of art transforms physical things like paint for painting but also the surface being used: wood, canvas and the like, and the object being used to put the paint on: brush, spatula, stick or whatever. Part of the fun and mystery of painting is discovering what the materials can do. The great painter Rembrandt discovered how to make paint look like light and shadow. A lot of modern art has played with paint and the means of putting it on. Jackson Pollock invented a way of creating textures and rhythms by using different ways of dripping paint on to a surface.

As well as paint, Jackson Pollock used sand to create texture in his paintings.

Transforming ideas

Some art transforms art that has already been there. (Some say that all art does this but that's another matter!) Take the Harry Potter books: a lot of the scenes or moments in the books are a bit like scenes and moments in other books – the idea of a boarding school where a little group of pupils get up to mischief or face danger; the idea of a school that trains people to do magic, and so on. JK Rowling transformed these to make something new. Take any Shakespeare play: he took stories that were already in old books – as with '*Romeo and Juliet*' – and he wrote plays using the plots or scenes from those old stories, but made them his own in creative ways.

Transforming experience

Some would say that all art transforms experience. That means that any artist uses and distils their feelings about their life and the times they live in, in whatever art they make. That's why we might say that the way we dance expresses the way we are and the way we think and feel – self-assured or shy, cautious or carefree, perfectionist or slapdash, and so on. This is why we call a lot of art 'self-expression'. Not all art is about expression of the self, though. A lot of it comes out of co-operation and collaboration: think of bands, orchestras, plays, films. The '*Toy Story*' animated film series, for example, comes out of the work of hundreds of people. When we make art together – as with a school play – we are transformed by discovering how we can or can't co-operate. We may well get to find out things about ourselves that we didn't know before!

The reader, watcher, listener

But what about the other end? The reader, watcher, listener – the receiver? This person brings their life experience to the art and responds. They are made sad, or happy. Or they are puzzled, disturbed, made anxious, say. Or they are delighted and feel stronger, perhaps. When we are affected by art, we can choose just to have that feeling and leave it at that, or we can ask questions of ourselves.

Think About

Next time you are affected by art, you could ask yourself questions like this:

- Why did I think that?
- How and why did my feelings change as I looked or read?

"We need that thing, where you leave a theatre feeling better than when you arrived."

*Sandi Toksvig,
writer and performer*

Where do we find art?

The word 'art' itself sometimes makes us think immediately of paintings on the wall in big galleries in cities around the world. Yes, that is one place to find art, but when we remember that the word means much more than that, we can find art everywhere.

Official art and secret art

In fact, every society known to us has made art of one sort or another. Sometimes it's very public and official: all over the world when chiefs, kings, queens and rulers are presented to the people or when they get married or die, music is played. But alongside this kind of art, there are more secret kinds of art. If you go into some churches in Europe, you might find funny, rude carvings under the choir seats, of such things as a monkey carrying a purse, or a naked man crawling along the ground.

In many places in the world, there have been rules about what can or can't be said about religion, politics, family life and so on. Quite often, this leads people to create a

The Kingdom Choir sang at the wedding of Prince Harry and Meghan Markle.

secret literature of pamphlets, songs, poems and jokes. These are often satirical, that is, they mock those in power, or highlight injustice, like the graffiti art, opposite (see pages 32-33).

Art and children

Another kind of art happens with very young children. If you watch them, you'll see them making up dances and songs, and plays for their toys. This role play helps children understand how the world works, and work out how they would like to fit into it.

Graffiti on walls ...

All over the world, people do graffiti. Sometimes these are multi-coloured graphic images or ornate lettering. Into this tradition came an artist known as Banksy. Secretly, he goes somewhere and uses stencils to make an image on a wall. Quite often these are funny pictures which mix up an image taken from one sphere of life with an image from another sphere, but they are always thought-provoking. Strictly speaking, what he does is often illegal – he's putting paint on somewhere that doesn't belong to him. Because it's so secret, it's called underground art, although it's nearly always put somewhere really visible like on a wall in a high street. Many graffiti artists, including Banksy, have a serious purpose to their art (see image below and pages 32-33).

... and in other places

You can also find more official sculptures in places where people can interact with them. On a beach in Suffolk, there's a shell-like sculpture made by Maggi Hambling called 'The Scallop', that adults and children can sit on and climb over (see page 4). In Shanghai, China, an artist called Huaibing Guan made a maze-like structure with paths inside. People can go through the paths to experience travelling in time. And in Perth, Western Australia, Geoffrey Drake-Brockman created a tall, interactive artwork called Totem, which responds to the movements of pedestrians and is sensitive to environmental conditions.

Art is everywhere.

Try This

Another place to find art is on our computers and phones. Use your phone or computer to:

• Take photos, make videos, edit films and make music;

• Make music using keyboards, guitars, or any other instrument.

Then record and share what you have created.

Banksy drew this image on the Separation/Apartheid Wall in Bethlehem in the Occupied West Bank. It shows two children playing with sand, buckets and spades on piles of rubble that look like sand, with a hole in the wall revealing an image of a beach that lies about 70 kilometres away, and that they are not allowed to visit.

My experience

Lemn Sissay

Lemn Sissay, MBE, is a BAFTA-nominated award-winning writer, poet, performer, playwright, artist and broadcaster. He has read on stage throughout the world. His acclaimed memoir *My Name Is Why* was published by Canongate Books in 2019.

Why did you start writing poetry?

To understand the world and myself better. I found that the imagination was a limitless, boundless space for me to inhabit. And the only rules were the ones that I made up. At the time, I was in children's homes where all the rules were made by detached adults.

Art saved my life. I cherished the world of the imagination as a new home, and I felt that once I had inhabited that world, this world had changed. If you create a world for yourself and inhabit it on the page, it changes the world around you. For example, imagine a world without Harry Potter, or Tracy Beaker, or Peter Pan, or Oliver Twist. The very act of creativity means that you can change the world one poem at time. Imagine that, all through a pen!

Poetry is an exploration

People often say to me that poetry is an escape, but I think of it as an exploration. I wasn't *escaping* from life. I was *exploring* life. I wasn't running away from reality. I was inhabiting myself and this other world of the mind. I found that incredibly empowering.

When you read a book, pictures emerge in your mind – a magical process. But the beautiful thing about your own creativity is that you might not know what it is you're going to say, write or paint until you've done it. It's like being a magician pulling a rabbit out and finding that it's not a rabbit but a lion, and you've got it by the ears. And look – out of our discussion we now have a new image, of a lion coming out of a top hat!

Poems as pebbles

The beauty of the imagination is that it can reflect on real life. My poems are like Hansel and Gretel's pebbles in the fairy tale. They make me remember my journey. I see in time and space where I was, who I was with, what I was going through at the time I wrote them. That was very important to me because I was in children's homes, and people were always coming and going – children every few days or weeks, staff every four hours. But I can look at a poem and know where I was. They don't have to refer to the place or time, but I remember.

Said the sun to the moon
Said the head to the heart
We have more in common
Than sets us apart

How do you do it said night
How do you wake and shine
I keep it simple said light
One day at a time

Why do we need art?

The reason we put pictures on the walls is that we want to see other worlds. That's why we read books, go to the cinema, listen to music – all these are explorations. All these are art. Just look around you and see how many pieces of art there are: the designs on your bed covers, your birthday card, food packaging, the art in songs. Art is all around us.

Now try to imagine a world without art. Look at those posters, the films you've seen, the books you've read, the songs you listen to. Then imagine a world where you could never hear a song or watch a film, never read a book. Then you'll know how important art is.

The importance of creativity

Creativity is the lifeblood of art, and it begins in you. You can't buy creativity from a shop. All you have to do to ignite your creative spirit is to try a poem or a drawing or even a splodge of colour! And that can start you off.

"Art saved my life."

Do you need training to become an artist?

As we've said elsewhere, we can all be artists, and in one way or another we all are and always have been.

Art that requires training

Of course, some kinds of art need training and practice – sometimes a lot of it. Here are some examples: jazz soloist, ballet dancer, portrait painter, ceramicist, feature film actor.

In many countries there are special schools and colleges where you can train in different ways to be an artist, like the BRIT School (which provides education and vocational training for the performing arts, media, art and design and the technologies that make performance possible), the Royal College of Art and the National Film and Television School in London, the Julliard School of dance, drama and music in New York, the Bunka Fashion Graduate University in Tokyo.

The artist known as Lady Gaga studied at New York University's Tisch School of the Arts before leaving to pursue a career in music.

Other ways

There are other ways to train and practise, though. Quite a few musicians teach themselves, join a band, teach themselves some more and practise for hours every day. Some very famous music – like that of the Beatles – was produced this way.

Another way is to go to university and develop your art 'on the side'. This is what Michael Rosen did (see page 10). He studied English Language and Literature at university while he wrote plays and poems, acted and directed in the theatre. Sometimes, the way art works is that different parts of your life join up in ways that you can't predict. For example, several famous musicians such as John Lennon, Ian Dury and Freddie Mercury went to art school.

It's usually very competitive to get into the top colleges of the arts. To get in you have to show that you're good, but you also need the character and persistence to succeed. After all, trying to make a living in the world of the arts is not like doing a job where there's a standard path you can follow. You have to be able to convince people that what you do is worth paying for!

So the training in these colleges can be quite challenging and rigorous.

They also bring you face to face with one of the great problems of the arts: what's it worth?

How is the value of art decided?

Why is it that one painting might be worth millions of pounds and another one, nothing? Why might one actor be paid millions of pounds to appear in a Hollywood film and another actor find it difficult to earn a living anywhere? Why will a publisher pay one writer a million pounds to write a book and another writer a few hundred?

There are at least two ways to answer these questions: one is to do with what the critics say, and the other is to do with the choices made by those who buy the art.

Every art has its critics. They go to exhibitions, concerts, plays, read books, go to galleries. Then they comment on the arts on TV and the radio, in newspapers and magazines. Over time, the voices of these critics may praise an artist or ignore them. Sometimes the artists win prizes such as the Oscars or the Turner Prize; there are hundreds of these all over the world. The combination of the criticism and the prizes can create fame and success.

The audiences

Meanwhile, there are people who will pay to see or hear the art, either by going in millions to see a film, or pay millions to buy a painting. This is known as the market, and anyone in the arts knows that if they want to live by their art, they have to take notice of this market; they have to be aware of who's buying what.

But art has more than just commercial value. As we've been saying, there are more enriching ways in which art has value. Let's look at what we gain by being creative.

Think About

Some works of fine art sell for huge amounts of money. What do you think of this?

At Christie's auction house in New York, USA, in 2017, a painting described as 'the last da Vinci' sold for a record-breaking US$ 450 million.

What use is the imagination?

What is the imagination?

Imagination is the basis of creativity. It's the ability of the mind to visualise or experience things you can't actually see in front of you, to see or experience with your 'mind's eye' something that you haven't experienced in reality. Perhaps we can think of it as a more intense way of seeing the world around us.

When we talk about imagination in this way, we're not talking about making up things that aren't true, we're talking about allowing our minds to roam freely, to see what they come up with. Sometimes what comes is strange and wonderful, and sometimes it might be dull and boring, but if we give ourselves the chance to daydream, rich and interesting ideas will come, as well as more ordinary ones.

Imagination can be transformed into something other by action – writing, drawing, dancing, painting.

"… that's what I find very special about contemporary dance: you have the possibility to imagine what it is for you, personally."

Dancer Akram Khan, in an interview for the Dumbo Feather website in 2012

What's the point of daydreaming?

The writer Philip Pullman says that imagination is one of our highest faculties, and when it's most intense it becomes a way of seeing and a state of mind, as in William Blake's poem in which we can "see a World in a Grain of Sand / And a Heaven in a Wild Flower". If we let ourselves daydream, we can find different worlds, ideas and images.

SIR STEVE MCQUEEN

A British artist, film director and screenwriter, Sir Steve McQueen has won many awards for his art, including an Academy Award and a BAFTA, and the Turner Prize for visual art. Talking about his experience of primary school, he said: "It was incredible. The friends I had, and the potential, the possibilities. Playing, drawing, the kinship of friends, experimenting, getting wet in the rain. I had the chance to daydream."

LEONARDO DA VINCI

Leonardo is one of the most famous artists of the Renaissance (late fifteenth and early sixteenth centuries), and is regarded as a creative genius. As well as his paintings, drawings and sculptures, he was also interested in architecture, science, music, mathematics and inventions. Many of the designs he sketched for a flying machine anticipate the modern aeroplane.

Imagination and science

Without imagination, science wouldn't come up with new discoveries, ideas and inventions that sometimes seem completely absurd at the time, but turn out to be inspired and lead to fundamental changes in society. An example of this is the discovery of electricity (see page 29).

There are many other people who have made inventions and discoveries that resulted from imaginative thinking. Here are just two – find out what you can about them and others.

Albert Einstein (see page 5) – developed the revolutionary theory of relativity in the early years of the twentieth century. His theory transformed theoretical physics and astronomy, and also led to practical results in engineering, for example in the development of satellite technology.

> ## "Logic will get you from A to B. Imagination will take you everywhere."
>
> ## "Knowledge is limited. Imagination encircles the world."
>
> *Albert Einstein*

Marie Skłodowska Curie (below) made important discoveries in the field of radiation and X-rays. She won the Nobel Prize for Physics and a few years later won another, for Chemistry – the only person to win the Nobel Prize in two different scientific fields.

My experience

Preti Taneja

Preti Taneja was born and grew up in the UK. Her parents came from India in 1968. Books were very important and as a child Preti spent a lot of time reading at home and in her local library. She has taught writing in prisons, made films with people in refugee camps and reported on the refugee crisis in the Middle East. *We That Are Young*, her first novel, was published in 2017; it has won literary prizes and been translated around the world.

What does art and being creative mean to you?

I see art everywhere. For a writer, everything is a possible image or a story – from a pigeon nesting in the cracks of a concrete underpass, to a girl from a village in India, working to save her people from climate disaster. Art is the realisation that things are always a representation of other things – even a plastic bag hung in a frame could represent something about the nature of our lives right now.

To me, being creative isn't a choice: it's something we can't help. When we sit down to make art, we are trying to do the most human of things: say what we think is important to say in our own way, in our own voice. If any of your early memories include drawing scribbles on paper, or on a wall, you will know what I mean.

Art in precarious places

I have worked in refugee camps and in slum areas in different parts of the world, in some of the poorest parts of Britain and in high security prisons, as well as in elite universities. Everywhere, there are people who want to make art. No matter who you are, you have the right to make art, not just consume art by someone else.

Art and refugees

No one ever aspires to become a 'refugee'. The people who flee conflicts or climate emergencies have professions and jobs – they might be artists, office workers, hairdressers, doctors. Many are children, living in very harsh conditions, but dreaming of what they might become. If they end up in camps, sometimes forcibly separated from their families, there's not much to do. Art can change that. It can show the people around you what you're all about and remind you of that too. Making art, you will surprise yourself. And looking at art, reading, listening or watching it, you might understand others and this world more deeply.

In prisons

Our society is unequal and our prison population reflects that. Although Black, Asian and Minority Ethnic people make up only 14 per cent of the UK population, they make up a quarter of the prison population. There are complex and interacting reasons for this, including historic discrimination in education and employment based on class, race and gender. Austerity has deprived working-class communities of access to the arts, including closing libraries and youth centres, so young people have nowhere to go except onto the streets. Other factors contribute, like negative stereotypes and racist policing.

But, if someone ends up in prison for a serious crime – does that mean they shouldn't make art?

Art enhances our concentration and sense of self-worth. It's not only about what gets produced at the end, but the thrill of making it. Some of the most powerful poetry I have read was written by people in prison, like this poem by JD Magwitch.

Un-bend your back
Un-bow your head
Clench your quivering jaw.
You have survived your darkest days
Now life demands some more.

Un-doubt your doubt,
Un-fear your fear,
Reset your focus straight.
Defend the weak:
Protect the poor:
Decimate the hate!

JD Magwitch

"Art ... can show the people around you what you're all about and remind you of that too."

What do we gain by being creative?

The individual

We can answer this question at several levels. Let's start with an individual person. Being creative is a way of thinking about how we live. We can go through life thinking of what we do as something given to us: school, work, TV, music, sport. It's just there! This is what might be called a 'passive' way to think of the world, where there's nothing the individual can do about it or with it. This way, you don't see yourself as part of anything that can change, and you may well see yourself as somebody who can't change their own life. That said, some people feel comfortable thinking like that.

Another way to think about how we live, is to see yourself as someone who can make and do things in creative ways. To feel free in many different parts of your life without fear of failing, not beaten down if things don't immediately work out. This might apply to any part of life: how you choose your clothes and do your hair to how you decorate your room.

Doing any of these things, finishing it and seeing how it makes other people happy, is a deeply satisfying thing to do. It's partly because we feel affirmed through other people being pleased with what we've done. But it's also because we have a sense of our own capabilities, our own power to change materials, and use our mind to transform experience (see pages 16-17).

> " ... for me, the basis of art is love. I love life."
>
> *Artist David Hockney*

During 2020's pandemic lockdown, children created pictures of rainbows to convey their thanks to key workers in hospitals, shops and schools. Bears appeared too, inspired by We're Going on a Bear Hunt!

Society

Another way to look at what we gain from creativity is to ask: What does society gain from our creativity?

There's plenty in this book about the pleasure people get from making and receiving the arts. But creativity is not confined to the arts. We often think of science as the opposite of the arts, and some people might say that the arts are about feelings whereas science is about facts. This is true only up to a point. Science works by trying to prove that certain things are true or false. The arts don't usually try to prove anything is true, but they often try to show that something feels true, or that it has integrity or honesty. Slightly but not completely different!

But then again, for science to get to the point of trying to prove something is true, it has to try out several or many possibilities first. This is where something more like the arts creeps in.

ALESSANDRO VOLTA AND ELECTRICITY

For a long time, scientists thought that electricity was something that came from animals – including us. They didn't know that it could travel from one piece of metal to another along a third piece of metal, like a wire.

The big breakthrough happened when an Italian scientist called Alessandro Volta played with bits of metal and a piece of foil in his mouth! He put one kind of metal on top of his tongue, and another kind of metal under it, and joined them together with a bit of foil. He felt a tingle. But when the two bits of metal were not joined by the foil – there was no tingle. He discovered that the mix of the saliva in his mouth, and two different kinds of metal being joined, produced what we now call an electric charge.

Was this art? Designing his experiment was in its way artistic, and it was certainly creative, full of imagination and planning, mixed up with the science of trying to prove something.

And the world changed! Look around you and see how much relies on electricity going down wires.

This kind of creative thinking – imaginative, experimental, not worrying about failure, and in its own way, artistic – will be needed to solve the world's problems of climate change, poverty and disease.

My experience

Peter Beard

Peter Beard has been an artist for over 40 years, working mostly in ceramics but also in bronze. He exhibits internationally and his work has won many awards and is included in many museums and public and private collections.

Art and emotion

For me, art, in all its forms, speaks to the soul of the human being. Whether it is literature, painting, sculpture, video or music, it engages our emotions as nothing else does. It raises us above simply existing as living beings, as part of the wider animal world.

I believe that every one of us is born as a creative person. Creativity begins with thought and imagination. We are each individual and unique and our daydreams can become tangible objects if we give them free rein. We may not know it at the time, but when we begin scribbling with crayons as babies, we are expressing our creative selves, free of inhibition. As we grow older, the practicalities of surviving day to day can inhibit our creative urge and constrain us. This means we have less time to explore our instinctive curiosity about how we can express our feelings about the world around us.

My work

I am always thinking about my work, whether it is ideas I am already working on or influences that appear in the wider environment. It is difficult to remember everything so I always carry a sketchbook, large or small, so that I can jot down ideas.

For me, beginning to make a new piece of work is the most exciting part of my creative process because there is anticipation of what is to come. Seeing the final result when the kiln is opened is also an exciting moment. Success or failure is revealed – joy or disappointment. Disappointment provokes the desire to do better.

Differences in the thickness of glaze application result in differences in colour – and the outcome can be disappointing (or surprisingly nice). Occasionally, pieces crack but somehow this is less of a disappointment because it's a technical problem that can be overcome.

I used to think that if I became successful and established my life would be easier. But both I and the public have expectations about what I will achieve next. So, life is not easier, but remains very rewarding.

What does creativity do for us?

At its most basic level, creativity provides an outlet for a person's desire to express individuality, to have control over one's life either as part of a team or as a solo creator and to experience a true sense of reward and satisfaction. I am fortunate that my ideas are appreciated by the wider world and I make my living from my ceramics, but it matters not whether your ideas are liked by others or not, the fact that you express yourself makes the creative person grow in stature and experience a personal satisfaction like no other.

> "... creativity provides an outlet for a person's desire to express individuality ..."

Techniques

We asked Peter about how he makes his pieces. He told us:

"I have two techniques – wax resist and ground work, either thrown or hand built.

"Wax resist work is fired in a kiln, then a layer of glaze is applied. Patterns are painted with wax on top of this layer. Further layers of glaze are applied and the wax acts as a resist. The piece is fired again, the glazes melt, the wax burns away and the piece is finished – the 'frame' in the photo (right) is a disc made this way."

"With ground work, thin layers of coloured clay are built up to a depth of about 1 cm. The piece is fired and glazed several times and finally the surface is ground back using diamond tools to reveal intricate patterns and colour built up in the structure. They are textured but have a silky surface – the piece I'm holding was made this way."

Can art speak truth to power?

Is art powerful enough to be a threat to those in power? The answer to that is yes. You just have to see where and when different kinds of art – including visual art, drama, fiction and religious art – have been banned or censored throughout history and across the world. Places include China today, as well as Nazi Germany before and during the Second World War.

A Black Lives Matter protest in San Francisco, USA, in 2020, used different forms of art to commemorate the life of George Floyd who was killed by a police officer. Demonstrations like this were organised all over the world.

Art as a threat

For art to be banned or censored, the authorities must believe that it is powerful in some way, that it's a threat, that it will cause people experiencing it to disagree with, or disobey, those in charge.

Some art explicitly encourages people to protest and disobey, for example posters calling on people to take part in anti-government demonstrations. Other forms seek to persuade in more subtle ways – by getting people to imagine a different way of living or thinking. Or by simply showing the results of war or oppression.

WHAT IS SATIRE?

Satire, particularly political satire, is a form of art that aims to draw attention to certain issues in society, by making fun of individuals, groups or governments, challenging their pronouncements and examining them for hypocrisy, or for not supporting their claims with evidence.

The comedian Sarah Cooper satirises President Trump's statements in press conferences, such as when he suggested injecting disinfectant as a possible treatment for coronavirus. She does this by lip synching a recording of his exact words. The videos Cooper has made have been viewed by millions on social media. She says: "It is a very validating thing to see something remind you that, no, this is actually ridiculous and we can all agree on that."

You can find examples of satire in newspapers, magazines, social media and online.

It is often used as a way of undermining authoritarian regimes, through underground magazines or graffiti, when political speech and other forms of dissent are forbidden.

Attempts to control art

Find out what you can about these situations where art, including books and music, has been censored or even destroyed.

- The banning or censoring of books (such as the Harry Potter series) in schools in some parts of the USA.

- China and North Korea today: what is censored?

- Fascist Italy and Nazi Germany (destroying 'decadent' art).

- Puritans in seventeenth-century Europe smashing religious icons.

- The USA and South Africa banning jazz during segregation and apartheid.

- The destruction of the Bamiyan statues and other art in Afghanistan.

AI WEIWEI

This photo shows the Chinese artist Ai Weiwei visiting a refugee camp at the Greek-Macedonian border in 2016. The artist and outspoken critic of the Chinese government was arrested by the Chinese authorities in 2011 for 'economic crimes' and kept in prison for 81 days without charge. He has since made artworks depicting his experience of being in prison.

Can art change anything?

Art does not show us what to do. It hands us the responsibility to decide for ourselves how we respond to it. This in itself may change perception and lead to action of some kind, which leads to change. Art can change the way we think, it can influence us, make us think again about things we took for granted. It can even give us hope.

Here are two examples of artists who use their work to make people think, with the aim of making them change their behaviour.

MAKING PEOPLE THINK ABOUT RACISM

Akram Khan, MBE, is an English dancer and choreographer of Bangladeshi descent. He made a documentary for Channel 4 in 2019, '*The Curry House Kid*', about his experience growing up, which includes a dance piece that he created for the film.

This was written about the film: "In the Brick Lane boxing club where British-Bangladeshi boys taught themselves to fight racism in the 70s, he takes to the ring

and through a series of rising and falling movements distils the terror and shame of racism into dance."

Watching the film, a student at the nearby Mulberry School for Girls, said: "Dance does the things that you cannot speak about."

MAKING PEOPLE THINK ABOUT CLIMATE CHANGE

Olafur Eliasson is an artist who strives to make the concerns of art relevant to society at large. For him, art is a crucial means for 'turning thinking into doing'. This was the impetus behind Ice Watch, an installation consisting of twelve large blocks of ice cast off from the Greenland ice sheet. Eliasson, and geologist Minik Rosing, wanted to make the climate explicit, so that people could understand the reality of climate change – to see, touch and relate to the ice, and watch it slowly melt, to understand that this is what is melting and disappearing through climate change.

Ice Watch outside Tate Modern, London.

> "Put your hands on the ice, listen to it, smell it, look at it – and witness the ecological changes our world is undergoing."
>
> *Olafur Eliasson*

Can art help change how we feel?

Art can offer people who are having to cope with difficulties or trauma in their lives a route back to connecting with others, such as young Palestinian adults living under occupation in very difficult circumstances, making dance, drama and poetry to express themselves. The charity Childline offers children access to an area on its website called Art Box. It's an outlet where children can safely communicate through art, things that they might find too traumatic to speak about. The website says: "Creativity can help you calm down or make sense of things."

My experience

Mathilda Crompton and Meri Wells

Mathilda Crompton was born in 2007 in Bristol, and now lives in a remote part of mid Wales. She participates in a project called "Criw Celf" (meaning "Art Group" in Welsh), which takes students across Wales to meet artists.

What art means to me

When I am upset, art calms me down. After arguing with my brother, all I need is a pencil and a piece of paper to cheer myself up. Almost all of my life revolves around my imagination. There is so much potential in a blank page. All the famous paintings in the world began with an empty canvas. It's our job as artists to fill that space, and to give it life. A white page isn't just nothing: it's everything.

Daydreaming

When I was small, I read books about young girls who daydream, and I wanted to be like them. The girls would sit for hours, just thinking. I couldn't do this for more than a minute. Soon after I turned 12, I read *A Little Princess* by Frances Hodgson Burnett, and loved the way she would 'pretend' to be in a different world. I realised that you don't try to daydream, it just happens. I had unconsciously been asking myself questions, putting myself in impossible situations and, in effect, daydreaming. It's the same with art. If you try too hard to think of an idea for a painting or drawing, then no ideas will come. If you let the ideas come to you, however, you will not be disappointed. Now I know that, I don't draw half as much as I used to, but the drawings I create are a thousand times better.

> "... don't try to daydream, it just happens ... let the ideas come to you"

Meri Wells

Recently, Meri Wells invited me into her garden and studio. Walking into her studio was like walking into a scene from Lewis Carroll's *Alice in Wonderland*; it was full of interesting things: figures, skulls, mugs, stones. It helped me to understand that where an artist works is more than what it looks like on the outside. It is full of nothing and everything; it's a tidy mess.

Meri has an extremely queer way of looking at the world; she sees shapes in everything – a piece of wood with a nail through it is an angel, a rock is a demon. She sees magic in things that I saw as junk. She makes them into pieces of art. Legends. Stories. Songs. Each one has its own tale to tell. Each one is unique. The sculptures wore blank, disconcerting looks on their faces, and they made me feel uneasy. They had depth, as if they could see straight through me, but they were some of the most imaginative things I have ever appreciated properly.

Why do we need art?

Imagine what would it be like if art didn't exist. Our lives would be dull: no photographs, no paintings, no sculptures. This is because invention is a form of art. Everything made by human hands must have been invented at some point, so life without creativity would be rather empty, and unimaginably prehistoric.

MERI WELLS AND HER WORK

Meri Wells is a sculptor who works with clay. She says:

"I work alone in a tin shed in a narrow valley, with fields, hedges and woodland on the hill opposite. When I loosen my focus, I can see figures and faces in the ever-changing hedgerows, and these form a basis for my community of other beings processing through the by-ways of life. Someone said that the creatures – part human, part animal or bird – suggest emotions and tensions that lie under the surface of all human relationships. I'd like to think so.

"My figures evoke the shifting sense of ourselves as part of everything else. They break down the boundaries between us and the rest of nature. These animal creatures are more human than humans, haunting glimpses of our basic emotional existence."

'Refugees: queueing and waiting, at borders, for food – this is their life now.'
What human emotions do you see depicted in this sculpture?

Is comedy art?

One of the most popular things we do is watch and listen to comedy. In towns and cities across the world there are comedy clubs and comedy evenings where stand-up comedians try to make people laugh; there are comedy shows on TV and the radio, and films that are either comedies or have comic moments in them. There are hundreds of funny books for all ages as well as funny cartoons as single frame pictures, comic strips, or cartoon films.

But is it art?

Comedians and the makers of funny books and cartoons usually think so. They look at situations that many of us don't find funny and make them funny. They invent all sorts of situations for their scripts or performances, and something happens that makes us laugh. Physical comedy and mime are also art. The body is being used to tell a story, to make us laugh.

Think About

What are your favourite jokes? Can you see what the surprise is?

Try making up a joke.

A COMEDIAN ON COMEDY: RUFUS HOUND

The art of surprise

We asked the comedian Rufus Hound about how jokes work. He told us:

"Jokes are really just an extension of the art of surprise. Our brains love patterns, so when we think we know what's coming, but something switches, our brains register that the pattern is broken and – if the surprise is a pleasing one (and sometimes if it's not) – we laugh."

Scholars of comedy

Many comedians and comedy writers are like scholars of comedy, storing up jokes and funny situations in their notebooks. Roald Dahl's notebooks are full of moments that he invented, tricks that people might play on each other, so that he could use them in his books.

People were being artistic about comedy 400 years ago. In Shakespeare's time there was a clown, or fool, called Robert Armin. He wasn't the sort of clown we think of now, in clown's suit and red nose; he was one of the actors in Shakespeare's plays. There was often a character called the Fool, whose role was to make someone important laugh, but also to give them advice in a jokey way.

Robert Armin wrote books about comedy. He found that there are people who are naturally funny, like the kind of people you find amongst your family or friends, and then there are people who study how to be funny, inventing jokes and comedy. Robert Armin's art, like Shakespeare's, has lasted right through to the present day.

A COMEDIAN ON COMEDY: SHAZIA MIRZA

Why is comedy important?

We asked the comedian Shazia Mirza if she thinks comedy is art. She told us:

"Comedy is important to me because it's the purest and most direct way of talking about life, and it's the hardest and finest art form. Comedy is concise. Every line has a motive and a reason, it's leading somewhere, to a punchline of some kind. Comedians are observers – we stand on the outside of life and tell everyone what and how we see it. No one is more necessary than a comedian."

But what is comedy for?

Some people think that comedy is a way in which we can live in the moment without anything sad from our own lives troubling us. This might be true for some comedy, which can be thought of as escapist – whose purpose is to help us escape from our own troubles, or from the boring aspects of our lives. But comedy is also used very effectively to deal with great sadness, like grief or depression. Or to challenge stereotypes, for example about disabilities. There are many comedians, like Francesca Martinez and John Williams, who use those topics as the subject of their shows.

Why do we create music?

We nearly all make music of some kind, joining in with songs, humming, whistling, tapping our feet to a tune.

Some people do more than that, they make up songs and tunes, play musical instruments, play in bands, groups and orchestras. And some people compose complex pieces of music like concertos, symphonies, sonatas and the like.

But what's it for?

The composer Will Todd told us that he thinks music is to have fun with. And it's fun because it helps you to feel things, like being sad or jolly. Music vibrates sound. It not only creates the big rhythms made by the beat, it also creates tiny rhythms when, for example, the strings of a guitar or a violin make a musical note.

Music, says Will, takes you on a journey. It might be in steps or in surprising leaps, and when we listen, we follow it, leaping when the music leaps. And it's the same with rhythm: when it's slow, we feel slow; when it's quick and pounding we feel energetic.

Some music also works through harmony, when two or more notes are played or sung at the same time. You can do this by plucking two strings of a guitar at the same time, or pressing two keys on a keyboard. But why do different harmonies (or chords) make us feel different things? That might be, says Will, because of the tradition we've been brought up in, so some chords sound sad, others jangling or jarring.

Music in different cultures

Different cultures have different musical sounds and traditions, including different favourite harmonies, rhythms, notes and 'steps', so you go on different musical journeys with them.

The art of composers and musicians is to play with all these elements and create moods, feelings, surprises and journeys.

Varieties of music

As with all arts, there is a variety across the world right now. While you're reading this, you might stop for a moment and see if you can find music from different countries like, say, India, China, South Africa, Greece, Chile, and so on. And you can compare these with what we call Western music, by composers like Mozart or Benjamin Britten.

But there is a variety branching back into history too. Musicians can recreate the music from hundreds of years ago because it was written down. They can use old musical instruments or use new instruments made like the old ones.

Music through history

Down through history, creative musicians invented new sounds. For example, at the end of the nineteenth century, African American guitar players and singers developed a music we call the Blues, which uses notes and harmonies that have a sad sound.

At other times people invented opera, symphonies, jazz, string quartets, and instruments like bag pipes, trombones, sitars, didgeridoos, and a thousand more. In one lifetime, people in popular music can invent new styles. Since 1946 there have been styles like crooning, rock'n'roll, country and western, reggae, punk, hip-hop, heavy metal, rap, grime and many more.

Music is a hugely varied, ever-changing creative world where we can all find a music that suits us, instruments that we prefer, and sounds – rhythms, harmonies – that we like.

> **"I used to try to write lyrics whether or not I was in the mood, so it developed like a craft that I was obsessed with."**
>
> *George the Poet*

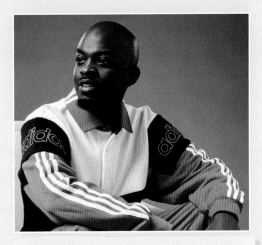

GEORGE THE POET

George the Poet is a London-born spoken word performer of Ugandan heritage. His innovative brand of musical poetry has won him critical acclaim both as a recording artist and a social commentator. He has also won numerous awards for his podcast 'Have you heard George's Podcast?', including a Peabody Award in 2020. The podcast provides a mix of drama, news, poetry, observations, lived experience, experimental ideas and music.

He talks here in an interview with Adam Buxton, about how he created a new form of music.

"I made grime when I first emerged as a rapper. I took an ideological stance quite early on. At 14 years old I was really curious about how we could tweak the formula so that everything that we are could be expressed in the music – we are all someone's friend and there is no violence, no machismo involved in that, we're just chill with people. I went down a different path with the content that I was creating at a very early age."

My experience

Kate Clanchy

Kate Clanchy is an award-winning poet, writer of novels and non-fiction, and teacher. She has published an acclaimed collection of poems written by the children she teaches, called *England: Poems from a School*, as well as a memoir looking back on her teaching career: *Some Kids I Taught and What They Taught Me*, which won the 2020 Orwell prize for political writing.

What is poetry for?

For the last 10 years, I've been Writer in Residence in my local, multicultural secondary school, writing poems with students of all ages and from all kinds of backgrounds.

When I tell older people this, they say things like *That must be hard. Teenagers don't like poetry, do they?* This makes me cross. My students are very positive about poetry and read lots of it, and so do teenagers in general – one survey in America recently found that poetry-reading among the under 25s had doubled between 2012 and 2017. I think people haven't noticed because teenagers are reading poetry differently – not from leather backed anthologies, but on their phones, and often in the form of an Instagram image, YouTube video, or Twitter post. Poems fit very well on phones: they are the right sort of shape, can be read in a few spare moments, and are so easy to pass on.

What are the teenagers finding in poetry?

Sometimes, just a joke – a rhyme or a neat phrase makes a comparison more memorable – and passing on wit has always been one purpose of poetry. Sometimes, it's something that helps them feel part of a group, or which stirs them to action: some of my most avid poetry readers come from poetry loving places such as Afghanistan or Syria; some of them like to read protest poetry.

" ... teenagers are reading poetry differently ..."

" ... each poem is an exchange."

Most often though, it's something very intimate, close to the heart, a poem by a stranger which seems like a text message from a friend. Poetry has always been able to communicate like this, because it is figurative and musical – it uses images and sounds, the irrational, uncountable, uncodified aspects of language – to communicate its meaning. Historically, poems have often been written in the form of letters or odes to particular people: now, they can be sent like text messages. Poems have always been a conversation – a special one, both public and private – and now teenagers are joining in using social media. Of course, not all the poems are brilliant – but most poems across time haven't been brilliant. We remember the few that are.

So, teenagers are expressing themselves in poems?

Yes, but that's not the only thing they are doing. When I read my students' poems I can see that their writing comes from their reading of poems, often very directly, as they borrow the form or shape of a poem that appeals to them. As they write, they pay attention to the shapes of their thoughts – their images – and the sounds of their language. They think about their reader, and how they will make the poem the best, most truthful, striking, forceful work they can. They think about how their words will look on the page. What my students say most often about writing poetry is not that they have 'expressed themselves' or 'got something out' but that they 'feel heard'. That's because they have joined in the great conversation of poetry and know that each poem is an exchange.

This poem demonstrates all the things poetry can be – accessible, personal, political, artful, memorable – and that 12-year-olds can write it.

The Word Ummi – My Mother

My beloved mother.
When I go to my house the pain of missing her
Arrives before me.

Mohamed Assaf (aged 12)

What do you think?

We have seen that art is all around us, part of our world. Our aim in this book is to show you what others think about the issues we've raised, but most importantly, it's to give you the opportunity to think about the issues for yourselves.

Think About

ART AND CULTURE

• What does art mean to you?

• Do you think human beings need art? Why or why not?

• What meanings or purposes can you find for art in other cultures?

COLLABORATION

• Have you ever made something with another person, or a group? It could be painting, drawing, writing, music, food or anything!

• How do your favourite bands make music?

• Do you know any other collaborative artists or artworks?

CREATIVITY AND CHANGE

• What do we gain by being creative?

• Can art change anything?

When we are affected by art, the feelings can often prompt questions in our minds, like:

• Why did I think that? How and why did my feelings change as I looked or read? What did it make me think of?

• How is this work made/written/ constructed?

HOW DO DIFFERENT FORMS OF ART MAKE YOU FEEL?

Engaging with art can transform us as readers, watchers and listeners. This new experience of the art goes into our minds like a new flavour we've added to a dish of food. You could say that absorbing a new work is like changing the taste of your mind!

"... culture is something that brings people together. That's the whole point, because it's about humans communicating with other humans about what it is to be alive."

Actor and art collector Russell Tovey

SONIA BOYCE

The artist Sonia Boyce is Professor of Fine Arts at Middlesex University, London and Professor of Black Art and Design at University of the Arts, London. Sonia emphasises collaborative work, and has worked closely with other artists. Her work involves a variety of media, such as drawing, print, photography, video, and sound.

Sonia grew up in a creative household (her mother was a keen dressmaker and her siblings made music) and she drew obsessively as a child. Encouraged by her art teacher, she went to life drawing classes at the age of 15 and began to think of 'being an artist' as a possible career.

As a young Black woman artist she found that 'the system hadn't anticipated me, or anyone like me'. She kept going, and aged 25 became the first Black female artist to have her work purchased for the Tate collection. In 2016 she was elected a Royal Academician, the first Black woman artist to be elected.

In a recent interview she said:

"There are serious questions about how people can come together, particularly when there might be tensions around differences. But through art it is possible."

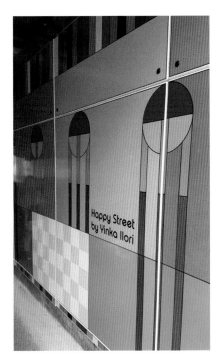

"Art doesn't give us life's answers as much as the power to live life's questions."

Actor Wendell Pierce

The artist and designer Yinka Ilori created 'Happy Street' as part of 2019's London Festival of Architecture, adding bright colour to the street architecture to make the environment more welcoming. He says: "Architecture and design should be for everyone, not just one group."

Over to you!

Try This

Here are some ideas for you to try. They might not all work for you, but you can think up some of your own.

- Go outside. Close your eyes and listen to all the sounds around you. What do you hear? Birdsong? Traffic noise? People talking? What does this do for you?

- Draw some doodles on a piece of paper. You can make lots of small ones, or you can embellish one and keep adding to it.

- Sketch a plan of your perfect room, home or school.

- Read a poem you like. Without thinking about it too much, write down the first line of the poem and continue the poem with your own thoughts.

- Close your eyes and think about a piece of art that you really like. What do you see in your mind's eye? What are the most striking things about it for you?

- Design a garden or decorate a cake/arrange food on a plate/flowers in a vase.

- Produce a short sketch for a friend's birthday.

- Make up songs or invent a dance routine.

- Design a poster for a cause that's important to you.

Thinking creatively about the future

Let's use our creativity to think about how we could reshape the future of the world. The experiences of the Second World War led to the creation of the National Health Service in the UK – an amazing, incredible feat of the imagination, set up for the social good.

How could we reshape our future?

Here are some ideas to think about. Which interest you the most? What topics could you add?

- Making the world a more equal place.

- Challenging, and eliminating, systemic racism.

- Energy, climate change and sustainability.

- Poverty and how to eliminate it.

- The fight against disease.

- Changing the way we think about our food and what we eat, including how food is produced and transported.

- New ways of planning cities and housing – around people rather than cars.

"Art is the highest form of hope."

Artist Gerhard Richter

Glossary

apartheid refers to a political system in which one group of people have full political rights, while others live separately with limited rights. First used to describe the former political system in South Africa

austerity a difficult economic situation caused by the government reducing the amount of money it spent, leading to cuts in funding for government funded institutions, including essential social services

censored/censorship removing something, such as a newspaper article, a book or a film that a government or other authority does not want people to see or hear

haiku a traditional Japanese poem written in three lines with seventeen syllables

occupation the settlement or taking and controlling of an area by military force; an act of possession against the wishes of the people who live there

segregation the policy of keeping one group of people apart from another and treating them differently, especially because of race, sex or religion

systemic a systemic problem is one experienced throughout the whole of an organisation or country, not just particular parts of it

> "The possible's slow fuse
> is lit by the imagination."
>
> *Poet Emily Dickinson*

Further Information

Some books and websites you might find interesting:

Books

Michael Rosen's Book of Play: Why Play Really Matters, and 101 ways to get more of it in your life, Wellcome Collection, 2019

My Name is Why, Lemn Sissay, Canongate, 2019

Some Kids I Taught and What they Taught Me, Kate Clanchy, Picador, 2019

These are the Hands: Poems from the heart of the NHS, anthology with Foreword by Michael Rosen, Fair Acre Press, 2020

We are Artists: Women who made their mark on the world, Kari Herbert, Thames and Hudson, 2019

Young Palestinians Speak: Living Under Occupation, Anthony Robinson and Annemarie Young, Interlink 2017

Websites

RSA (Royal Society for the encouragement of Arts, Manufacturers and Commerce (www.thersa.org). The RSA states on its website that it believes "in a world where everyone is able to participate in creating a better future, by uniting people and ideas to resolve the challenges of our time."

Arts Council England (https://www.artscouncil.org.uk) is a government-funded body dedicated to promoting the performing, visual and literary arts in England.

The Design Council (https://www.designcouncil.org.uk) describes itself as "an independent charity and the government's advisor on design." It says " Our vision is a world where the role and value of design is recognised as a fundamental creator of value, enabling happier, healthier and safer lives for all."

Katie Paterson (http://katiepaterson.org) is a conceptual artist. Much of her work is "rigorously scientific, but by presenting it through art she manages to bring out the more poetic aspects of the field." Particularly relevant for pages 24-25, on the use of the imagination.

Rethink (https://www.bbc.co.uk/programmes/p08gt1ry) is a series of radio programmes featuring leading thinkers from around the world who discuss how the world should change after the coronavirus pandemic.

Huaibing Guan – https://www.pinterest.fr/pin/464433780309026074/ - to see the interactive sculpture mentioned on page 19.

Geoffrey Drake-Brockman – https://www.drake-brockman.com.au - to see the interactive sculpture mentioned on page 19.

Index

Aboriginal 6
Afghanistan 33, 42
Andersen, Hans
 Christian 12
apartheid 33
architecture 4, 13, 25,
 45
Armin, Robert 39
Artists in Residence 15
audience 8, 10, 17, 23
Australia 6, 19
Azerbaijan 13

band (music) 9, 17, 22,
 40, 44
Banksy 18, 19
Bausch, Pina 12
Beard, Peter 30–31
Beatles, The 9, 22
Beyoncé 12
Bhutan 6
Bible 13
Black Lives Matter (BLM)
 movement 32
Boyce, Sonia 45
Breughel the Elder,
 Pieter 13
BRIT School 22

censoring (of art) 32, 33
China 19, 32, 33, 40
choir 8, 18
Clanchy, Kate 42–43
climate crisis 7, 26, 29,
 35, 46
collaboration 9, 14, 15,
 17, 44, 45
comedy 38–39
communication 8, 12,
 14, 15, 35, 43, 44
community 8, 9, 13, 14,
 15, 27, 37
cooking 4
Cooper, Sarah 33
coronavirus 7, 33, 46
creativity 4, 5, 7, 14, 20,
 21, 24, 29, 30, 31, 35,
 37, 44, 46

critics 23
Crompton, Mathilda
 36–37
culture 6, 8, 9, 40, 44
Curie, Marie Skłodowska
 25

dance 4, 7, 8, 12, 16, 17,
 22, 24, 34, 35, 46
da Vinci, Leonardo 23,
 25
design 4, 12, 13, 16, 21,
 22, 25, 45, 46
design, fashion 12
de Villiers, Sarah 13
Dickinson, Emily 47
disability 15, 39
Drake-Brockman,
 Geoffrey 19
Dury, Ian 22

Einstein, Albert 5, 25
Eliasson, Olafur 35
empathy 7
expression 8, 17

film 4, 5, 12, 17, 19, 21,
 22, 23, 24, 26, 34, 38

gallery 4, 12, 23
gardening 4
George the Poet 41
Germany 6, 32, 33
graffiti 18, 19, 33
Guan, Huaibing 19

Hadid, Zaha 13
Haim 9
Hambling, Maggi 4, 19
Harry Potter series
 (books) 17, 20, 33
history 7, 8, 15, 32, 41
Hockney, David 28
Hound, Rufus 38

identity 8
Ilory, Yinka 45

imagination 4, 5, 11, 20,
 21, 24–25, 29, 30, 36
India 7, 26, 40
indigenous 6, 7
internet 4, 7

Japan 6, 7

Kaskar, Amina 13
Khan, Akram 24, 34

Lady Gaga 22
Lennon, John 22
library 12, 26, 27
literature 4, 18, 22, 30
lyrics 9, 41

Martinez, Francesca 39
Master Quilters of the
 Gee's Bend, The 9
McQueen, Alexander 12
McQueen, Steve (Sir) 24
Mercury, Freddie 22
Mili, Gjon 9
Mirza, Shazia 39
museum 4, 12, 13, 30
music 4, 6, 7, 9, 12, 18,
 19, 21, 22, 25, 28, 30,
 33, 40–41, 44, 45
myth 13

nature 13, 37
North Korea 33

painting 9, 15, 16, 18,
 23, 24, 25, 30, 36,
 37, 44
pandemic 7, 28, 46
performance 10, 22, 38
Peters, Sally 8
photography 7, 45
Picasso, Pablo 9
Pierce, Wendell 45
poetry 4, 20, 27, 35, 41,
 42, 43
Pollock, Jackson 16
poverty 29, 46
prison 26, 27, 32

racism 34
refugees 11, 26, 32, 37
Richter, Gerhard 46
Rihanna 9
Rosen, Michael 10, 22
Rosing, Minik 35

satire 33
school 10, 11, 12, 14,
 15, 17, 22, 24, 28, 33,
 34, 42, 46
science 4, 14, 15, 25, 29
sculpture 4, 19, 25, 30,
 35, 37
segregation 33
Shakespeare, William
 12, 17, 39
Sissay, Lemn 20–21
South Africa 13, 33, 40
storytelling 6, 7, 10

Taneja, Preti 26–27
teacher 5, 10, 12, 14,
 42, 45
theatre 4, 8, 12, 17, 22
Todd, Will 40
Toksvig, Sandi 17
Tovey, Russell 44
training (art) 22–23

United States of
 America (USA) 9, 23,
 32, 33

Vally, Sumayya 13
value (of art) 23
values 8
Volta, Alessandro 29

Wells, Meri 37
Weiwei, Ai 33
West Bank 19
Williams, John 39
Williams, Pharrell 9

Young, Annemarie 11

Zafirakou, Andria 14–15